Bellybutton Fuzz

and Other Poems to Ponder

by Ronnie Sellers
illustrated by Jon Davis

SELLERS
PUBLISHING

Published by Sellers Publishing, Inc.
Copyright © 2021 Sellers Publishing, Inc.
Illustrations © 2021 Jon Davis
All rights reserved.

Sellers Publishing, Inc.
161 John Roberts Road, South Portland, Maine 04106
Visit our website: www.sellerspublishing.com • E-mail: rsp@rsvp.com

Charlotte Cromwell, Production Editor

ISBN 13: 978-1-5319-1482-0
Library of Congress Control Number: 2020943719

No portion of this book may be reproduced, stored in a
retrieval system, or transmitted in any form or by any means,
mechanical, electronic, photocopying, recording, or otherwise,
without the written permission of the publisher.

10 9 8 7 6 5 4 3 2 1

Printed in China.

Contents:

Dedication:

To Lindsey Sellers, who has, since he was a boy,
reminded me that fun should be a priority,
and without whom these poems might
never have been written.

Introduction

A poem serves a noble cause
And has throughout all time.
It brings the written word to life
With rhythm, sound and rhyme.

The poems that comprise this book
Are doggerel, no doubt.
But still, perhaps they'll help convey
What language is about.

I hope the children reading them,
Whose lives have just begun,
Will see that words have beats and tones
And playing with them is fun.

Our language is a precious gift
That sets our kind apart.
A child who's taught a love for words
Will thrive right from the start.

Ronnie Sellers

Bellybutton Fuzz

Bellybutton fuzz. Bellybutton fuzz.
Don't know where it comes from.
Don't think anyone does.

Go to sleep at bedtime.
Bellybutton's nice and clean.
Wake up there's more fuzz in there
Than you have ever seen.

Bellybutton fuzz. Bellybutton fuzz.
Don't know where it comes from.
Don't think anyone does.

Brother says it comes from
The junkie food I eat.
Sister says a fairy puts the fuzz in while I sleep.
Don't know where it comes from.
Don't think I much care.
But, y'know, it's kind of fun to find the fuzz in there!

Bellybutton fuzz. Bellybutton fuzz.
Don't know where it comes from.
Don't think anyone does.

Ruth's a Goof

Ruth's a goof, and that's for sure.
She knows a hundred jokes or more.
She cracks me up. She's such a clown.
When I'm with Ruth I never frown.

She's got a hat shaped like a trout.
She takes it off and worms fly out.

Don't smell the flower on her shirt
Unless you want to get a squirt!

She'll make a rabbit disappear
Then pull a carrot from her ear!
I've lots of friends, and that's the truth.
My favorite, though, is goofy Ruth.

POP

Worry Warts

Listen to your Mama.
Listen to your Dad.
Never play out in the street
Or say words that are bad.

Don't cause any mischief.
Don't go near the tracks.
Never talk to strangers.
Always watch your back.

Zipper up your sweatshirt.
Tie your laces tight.
Stay where we can see you.
Come in while it's light.

Don't go in the puddles.
Don't get too much sun.
Now go play, enjoy yourself.
A kid deserves some fun!

Peter Picked a Python for a Pet

Peter picked a python for a pet
A choice poor Pete would soon come to regret.
The python grew as lengthy as a log
And swallowed up his neighbor's little dog.
When Peter heard the neighbor scream and shout

He quickly came to pull the puppy out.
But Peter's python fought a passionate fight
And wouldn't let Pete take his tasty bite.
So Peter tricked the snake, the story goes.

He put some pepper up the python's nose
And when the snake let out a giant sneeze
The dog blew out and landed in the trees.
The dog was fine, although a little sappy.

Its owner, though, was really quite unhappy.
So Peter gave the snake up for a cat.
He says it's best to just leave things at that.

The python's happy in a home that's new.
Pete visits him on Sundays at the zoo!

Where the Ocean Came From

A raindrop landed on my noggin
And ran down my forehead to my nose.
Then it dripped from my nose to my lip to my chin
And down to a puddle by my toes.
The puddle overflowed into the gutter

Where it joined with the gutter's swelling flow.
I followed the water to the bottom of the hill
To see where it would go.
The water rushed down to a river.

The river flowed into the sea.
So remember when swimming in the ocean waves
It all began with me.

The Bookworm

Leslie will tell you her favorite times
Are those spent alone reading stories and rhymes.
She reads in the morning while riding to school.
She reads while she floats on a raft in the pool.

She reads while she's eating her jelly and bread.
She reads in the bathtub. She reads in her bed.

She reads about butterflies, tigers and snakes.
She reads about cyclones, volcanoes, earthquakes.
She reads about comets that blaze through the sky.
She reads books explaining how airplanes can fly.

She reads some so often she knows them by heart.
She just loves to read and that's why she's so smart.

Eels and Snakes

I've heard it said that eels and snakes
Prove Mother Nature makes mistakes.
By mixing genes with too much haste
She made two beasts that are a waste.

Perhaps, they say, she worked too fast
Because she made these creatures last.
She wasn't clear. She needed rest
And so she wasn't at her best.

She took some shortcuts, some folks say,
Because she wanted time to play.
She left off legs, the story goes,
To save time making knees and toes.

And once she left off legs that day
She thought, "I'll just go all the way
And skip arms too. Yes, what the heck,
They'll just have heads and one long neck!"

To me, these beasts are works of art
And prove that nature's really smart.
They aren't mistakes. What's really true
Is they confirm what she can do
Is quite miraculous, quite profound,
And should amaze, impress, astound!

If you're inclined to disagree
With both hands tied, go climb a tree!
A snake can do this feat with ease
It needs no hands or arms or knees.

Or bind both legs and try to swim.
The end result might be quite grim!
An eel can swim with speed and grace
Then fold into a tiny space.

Yes, eels are magical. Snakes too.
They mean no harm to me or you.
So please be kind, re-think, reflect,
And treat these creatures with respect.

If You Should Bring a Ghoul to School

If you should bring a ghoul to school
Make sure it doesn't snarl or drool.
A snarling ghoul is just not cool
And scares the teacher, as a rule.

If you should ask a shark to tea
Don't seat it very close to me
Or I'll be nervous as can be
'cause sharks get hungry, don't you see?

If you should ask a bear to play
I think I might stay home that day.
I couldn't keep my fear at bay.
The bear might look at me as prey.

If you should bring a monster home
Make sure you call me on the phone
And you, my friend, will be alone.

Snakes Have Simplified Their Lives

Snakes have simplified their lives.
They're minimalists, yet still survive.
They don't need lots of food to eat.
They don't need shoes. They have no feet!
They don't need bathing suits to swim.
They don't buy jewelry on a whim.

They have no features to bedeck.
No fingers, ear lobes, wrists or neck.
They don't need 'stuff', and so they're free
To be the best snakes they can be.

The Cow

The cow is such a peaceful beast
So docile and demure.
It lives its life without regrets
Well balanced and secure.

Its countenance should be a guide
For those who harbor doubts
Or ponder abstract, fretful things,
Like, "What is life about?"

Its pasture is its paradise
It never goes to mass,
Or temples, mosques or synagogues
To pray for greener grass.

To cows, the world is fine as is.
They have but one intent.
To live within the here-and-now
And graze until content.

Snake Envy

I sometimes wish I was a snake.
When weary of myself I'd shake
My old skin off from head to toes
And step out someone no one knows.

Beware on One October Night!

When days grow short and nights grow long
The hoot owl sings an eery song.
Beware on one October night
Or you might get an awful fright.
Peculiar things just might occur
For autumn's when the spirits stir
And headless horsemen ride their mounts
Past ghostly queens and vampire counts.

All sorts of creatures walk the streets
Bedecked in gowns and long white sheets.
The jesters joke, the gypsies dance,
The dervish whirls into a trance,

The pirate wields his sabre sharp,
The siren plays her haunting harp.
A wolf, a ghoul, a large black cat,
A fearsome shark, a giant bat,

They all go out in search of sweets
And play their tricks to get their treats.
A truly otherworldly scene
One night a year, it's Halloween!

Every Creature Has Its Flaws

Every creature has its flaws
And snakes are no exception.
Serpents move with lightning speed
But just in one direction.

Snakes can't slither in reverse.
This fact is really true.
So if you see a snake, back up
And it won't bother you.

Betty Bought a Rutabaga

Betty bought a rutabaga
At her neighborhood bodega.
Put it in a cotton sack.
Brought it home upon her back.

"What's this bulbous thing you bought?"
Mother wondered, quite distraught.
"Not a turnip. Not a beet.
Is it something we can eat?"

"Yes, of course," young Betty said.
"I'll bake us rutabaga bread.
Rutabaga bagels too,
And tasty rutabaga stew.

Rutabaga fries for lunch,
That's a snack you'll love to munch.
Rutabaga soup with leek,
Creamy, smooth, and quite unique!"

"Yum," Mom said, "it's good. You're right!"
When tasting Betty's soup that night.
"I LOVE this rutabaga dish!
It's thick and sweet and SO delish!"

And rutabagas once a day
Will keep you healthy, people say.
So when you're in your own bodega
Buy yourself a rutabaga.

The Monster Underneath My Bed

"A Monster's underneath your bed,"
My older brother Rowan said
As I was turning off my light
About to go to sleep last night.
"His teeth are huge. His body's hairy.
When he roars he's super scary.
Be forewarned, don't wake that beast
Or you might be his midnight feast!"

I tiptoed 'cross my bedroom floor
And then I heard a low-pitched snore
As thoughts of monsters filled my head
And made my body shake with dread.

I slipped beneath the sheets and cover
Wishing I could call my mother
But I dared not make a peep
That might disturb the monster's sleep.
"I'll stay awake all night," I thought.
"I won't doze off. I won't get caught.
I'll lay here 'til the break of day
Then, like a mouse, I'll sneak away."

An hour went by, then two, then three.
In hour four, I had to pee.
I had to go. I couldn't wait.
"I'm dead," I thought, "I'm monster bait."
I slipped my feet down off the bed
And stepped onto a hairy head.
The monster moaned and came awake.
I felt the bed lift up and shake.

I ran across the bedroom floor
And crashed into the bathroom door.
I couldn't see. It was too dark.
And then I heard the monster bark.

The door swung wide and Mom ran in
Awakened by the deafening din.
"What's all the noise so late at night?"
She yelled while switching on the light.
"A monster's underneath my bed.
Stay back, Mom, or we'll both be dead!"

Mom sighed, "Calm down, that isn't true.
Your brother's played a trick on you!"
She pulled the cover with a yank
So I could see my brother's prank.
And there beneath the bed was Molly.
She's our neighbor's giant collie!

"Molly's here for just one night,"
My mother said, "she doesn't bite.
She likes it when you scratch her nose."
I did, and Molly licked my toes.
I climbed in bed, tired as could be
Then Molly jumped on top of me.
That night I slept just like a log
Beneath that hairy monster dog!

If All the World Were Opposite

If all the world were opposite
How different things would be.
The whales would fly up in the sky
While birds swam through the sea.

If all the world were opposite
Then things would all fall up.
We'd need to rotate upside down
To drink juice from a cup.

If all the world were opposite
We'd swim when it was cold
And ice skate when the lakes got hot
Grow young instead of old.

If all the world were opposite
We'd start meals with dessert.
A funny joke would make us cry.
We'd bathe in tubs of dirt!

If all the world were opposite
We'd go to school at night.
We'd eat our lunches in the dark
Then sleep when it got light.

If all the world were opposite
The Nos would all be Yesses.
Kids would keep their bedrooms clean
And parents would make messes.

If all the world were opposite
Some things might sure perplex us.
Instead of saying our ABCs,
We'd say our ZYXs.

If all the world were opposite
The kids would all drive cars
And moms and dads would ride on bikes
And play on monkey bars.

If all the world were opposite
Then kids would be in charge.
We'd make the world a better place
For people small and large!